A double surprise

"So, who wants to help me solve the mystery of the locked closet in Room 3B?" Harry asked.

"Me!" lots of us replied.

Miss Mackle smiled as she walked over to the intercom and called the librarian.

Juju climbed up on his ladder and sat down on his platform. He probably wanted to get a better view of our investigation. I knew that closet was everyone's exit from cabin fever.

Even Juju's.

What I didn't know was that our locked closet would bring two really big surprises! One for the whole class, and one just for me.

BOOKS ABOUT
HORRIBLE HARRY AND SONG LEE

Horrible Harry and the Ant Invasion
Horrible Harry and the Christmas Surprise
Horrible Harry and the Drop of Doom
Horrible Harry and the Dungeon
Horrible Harry and the Green Slime
Horrible Harry and the Holidaze
Horrible Harry and the Kickball Wedding
Horrible Harry and the Locked Closet
Horrible Harry and the Mud Gremlins
Horrible Harry and the Purple People
Horrible Harry at Halloween
Horrible Harry Goes to Sea
Horrible Harry Goes to the Moon
Horrible Harry in Room 2B
Horrible Harry Moves Up to Third Grade
Horrible Harry's Secret

Song Lee and the Hamster Hunt
Song Lee and the "I Hate You" Notes
Song Lee and the Leech Man
Song Lee in Room 2B

Horrible Harry
and the Locked Closet

BY SUZY KLINE

Pictures by Frank Remkiewicz

PUFFIN BOOKS

Special thanks to my editor, Catherine Frank, for her valuable help with this manuscript; to my husband, Rufus, for his many readings; to Ed Beausoleil, a hard-working custodian, for his helpful expertise with old closets, and in particular, the one I had at Southwest School in Torrington, Connecticut; and to my daughter, Jennifer, for her devoted work with my books.

PUFFIN BOOKS
Published by the Penguin Group
Penguin Young Readers Group, 345 Hudson Street, New York, New York 10014, U.S.A.
Penguin Group (Canada), 90 Eglinton Avenue East, Suite 700, Toronto, Ontario, Canada M4P 2Y3
(a division of Pearson Penguin Canada Inc.)
Penguin Books Ltd, 80 Strand, London WC2R 0RL, England
Penguin Ireland, 25 St Stephen's Green, Dublin 2, Ireland
(a division of Penguin Books Ltd)
Penguin Group (Australia), 250 Camberwell Road, Camberwell,
Victoria 3124, Australia (a division of Pearson Australia Group Pty Ltd)
Penguin Books India Pvt Ltd, 11 Community Centre, Panchsheel Park,
New Delhi - 110 017, India
Penguin Group (NZ), Cnr Airborne and Rosedale Roads, Albany, Auckland 1310,
New Zealand (a division of Pearson New Zealand Ltd)
Penguin Books (South Africa) (Pty) Ltd, 24 Sturdee Avenue,
Rosebank, Johannesburg 2196, South Africa

Registered Offices: Penguin Books Ltd, 80 Strand, London WC2R 0RL, England

First published in the United States of America by Viking,
a division of Penguin Young Readers Group, 2004
Published by Puffin Books, a division of Penguin Young Readers Group, 2005

15 17 19 20 18 16

Text copyright © Suzy Kline, 2004
Illustrations copyright © Frank Remkiewicz, 2004
All rights reserved

LIBRARY OF CONGRESS CATALOGING-IN-PUBLICATION DATA IS AVAILABLE.

Puffin Books ISBN 0-14-240451-9

Printed in the United States of America

Dedicated to my grandson,
Jacob Matthew DeAngelis,
a treasure.

It's a joy reading books and
making volcanoes with you!

I love you, Jake!
Grandma Sue

My Dear Reader:

When I was a teacher, I had a closet door that was locked for many years. My students and I always wondered what might be inside. I didn't find out until our old school was remodeled.

Two years ago, a reader sent me a cover illustration for my next book. She called it <u>Horrible Harry and the Mysterious Door</u>. It made me think about my old classroom. Maybe it was time for Room 3B to have a locked closet. As soon as I started typing the story, I discovered Harry loved the idea! So thank you, Ally Sundal at Von R. Butler Elementary in Santa Rosa Beach, Florida, for your inspiration! Keep reading and drawing!

♡ Love,
Suzy Kline

P.S. Some of the things in my old locked closet turn up in Room 3B's closet in this story!

Contents

The Locked Closet   1

The *Things* under the Door   7

Volcanoes in Room 3B!   13

Harry's Discovery   22

The Hole in the Closet   32

The Search Party
in the Attic   40

The Mystery Is Solved!   49

Appendix   65

The Locked Closet

My name is Doug and I'm in third grade. It's January, and Room 3B is a snow prison. All week our teacher has been saying those two *deadly* words:

Indoor recess.

Indoor recess.

Indoor recess.

Today was Thursday, and it was sleeting. We were inside for the fourth day in a row. Everybody had a bad case of cabin fever.

Except for my best friend, Harry. He can find something smelly or slimy or scary or gross even indoors. Everyone will tell you what's most important to Harry in Room 3B.

Horrible things!

When the recess bell rang, I walked over to the computer. I wanted to go to my favorite Web site, FactMonster.com, and look up knock-knock jokes.

Harry and Ida joined me.

"Who wants to play checkers?" Sidney yelled.

"There aren't enough red pieces," Mary complained. "Remember?"

"I can make some," Song Lee replied.

"Rats!" I groaned. "Our computer is frozen! Now what are we going to do?"

"We could watch JuJu," ZuZu suggested. ZuZu was a new student who joined our class last month. He had brought his tortoiseshell guinea pig, JuJu, with him. Six of us gathered around his cage.

He wasn't gnawing.

He wasn't drinking.

He wasn't climbing.

"Maybe if we stare at him long enough, he'll poop in the corner," Harry said.

"That's gross!" Mary scolded.

"It's cool," Harry insisted. "JuJu's poops are neat little round brown pellets."

"They're not even smelly," Song Lee added with a giggle.

"But JuJu isn't doing *anything,*" Sidney moaned. "He's not even pooping."

Harry looked at Sid's nose and grinned. "Hey, we could count the boogers in your schnozzola."

While everyone laughed, Sid shot back, "Very funny . . . *Harry, the canary!*"

Harry half smiled and then got serious. "Or . . . we could be detectives."

"Detectives? And solve what, Harry?" ZuZu asked.

"The biggest mystery in Room 3B."

Everyone stared at Harry. We knew he loved mysteries. Last Halloween he dressed up in a suit like Sergeant Joe Friday, the famous police detective on TV.

"What mystery?" Mary repeated.

Harry leaped to the closet door. *"This!"* he shouted. Then he rattled the black doorknob. "It's been locked all year."

"All year?" Miss Mackle joined in. "I think it's been locked for *years*. I never bothered with it because there's another closet next to my desk."

All of us took turns trying to open the closet, but the door didn't budge.

"So who wants to help me solve the mystery of the locked closet in Room 3B?" Harry asked.

"Me!" lots of us replied.

Miss Mackle smiled as she walked over to the intercom and called the librarian.

JuJu climbed up his ladder and sat down on the platform. He probably wanted to get a better view of our investigation. I knew that closet was everyone's exit from cabin fever.

Even JuJu's!

What I didn't know was that our locked closet would bring two really big surprises! One for the whole class, and one just for me.

The *Things* under the Door

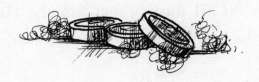

Indoor recess was exciting that day.

Our investigation got started with ZuZu's big question."What if the closet door is a fake?"

"What do you mean, Zu?" Dexter replied. "I know about fake Elvis Presleys, but not fake doors."

"Well, I read a story once about a closet that opened up to a brick wall."

"Oh, boo! I hope ours doesn't," Mary

groaned. "That would mean the end of our investigation."

Harry raised his eyebrows. "Let's find out." Everyone watched him take a piece of paper from his desk and get down on all fours. Very slowly, Harry slid the paper under the locked closet door.

"It went all the way in and out without crinkling!" ZuZu observed. "That means there's no brick wall!"

"Yahoo!" Mary shouted.

"Look at the space under the door," Harry pointed out. "It's big enough for a mouse to squeeze under."

Sid shivered.

Song Lee got a flashlight from our science tub, lay down on her side, and took a closer look.

"See anything?" Harry asked.

"Fuzzy things."

Harry borrowed Song Lee's flashlight and took a look. "They have to be dead fuzzy things. They're not moving."

Now Sid's teeth chattered.

Everyone watched Harry push the yardstick under the door. "Okay, Doug," Harry announced. "Give everyone a three-second warning. The *things* are coming out, dead or alive!"

No one moved.

I counted the seconds: "One hundred one, one hundred two, one hundred three . . ."

Harry swiped the yardstick across the closet floor like a windshield wiper.

All the *things* rolled out.

"*Yikes!*" Sidney yelled.

"*Whoa!*" we all exclaimed as we viewed the closet treasures on the floor.

Harry picked up our three missing red checkers and rattled them in his hand. Dust and hair fell through his fingers. "Someone probably kicked these under the closet door accidentally."

Sid snatched a broken candy cane that was still wrapped. "Mmmm," he said.

"Oh, goody!" Ida exclaimed. "There's my old rainbow barrette."

"And my postcard from Aunt Sun Yee in Korea!" Song Lee sang out. She blew off the dust, then held it close to her heart.

Mary made a face. "Just look at all those disgusting stub pencils and broken crayons!"

Harry rubbed his hands together. I knew he would find a use for them.

"Well, we found out what was under the closet door," ZuZu said. "Now we just need to find out what's on the shelves."

"*And* what's hanging on the hooks," Harry said with a toothy grin.

Mary just rolled her eyes.

Volcanoes
in Room 3B!

Brrrrrrrring! When the recess bell rang, we trudged back to our seats.

Miss Mackle was ready for our gloom and doom. "I don't think you'll mind an interruption from your detective work, if the *inter-ruption* is an *e-ruption!*"

Everyone looked at each other and shrugged.

"We've been studying rocks and

minerals for months. It's time, class, to add volcanoes!"

"I love volcanoes!" Harry blurted out.

"So why don't you marry one?" Sid joked.

Just as Harry held up a fist, Mrs. Michaelsen, the librarian, walked into our room. "You asked for all the books I had on volcanoes. Here are ten!"

"Thank you, Mrs. Michaelsen!" we all yelled.

"Have a *blast!*" she replied, waving good-bye.

"Okay, boys and girls," the teacher said. "Who wants to be a science detective and find ten facts about volcanoes?"

"Me!" we all roared.

Miss Mackle began drawing partners from her jar. "Mary and . . . Harry."

Harry sank down in his seat. Mary blew her bangs up in the air.

I was happy I got Song Lee for a partner. She's never bossy, and she works hard. As soon as we picked out our book, we got to work. We wrote down our favorite facts. There were more than ten. We even drew a big picture of the three kinds of volcanoes with different shapes.

When we brought our work up to the teacher, she said, "Great job! Let's go over to the sink and get started on your volcano. We can use this empty juice bottle."

Song Lee measured water, baking soda, and dishwashing detergent. I added drops of red food coloring. Then I poured in the white vinegar.

"Whoa!" Song Lee and I exclaimed

as the red liquid flowed down the sides of the juice bottle like lava.

Everyone had a turn to make an eruption before lunch except Harry and Mary. They didn't finish their research until after lunch. Harry had to listen to Mary read *every* word of their volcano book. And she insisted they recopy their facts for neatness.

Miss Mackle clapped her hands when they showed her their facts. "What neat work! Yahoo! But I'm sorry to say I've run out of white vinegar. We'll have to do your explosion tomorrow."

"Tomorrow?" Mary's eyes got watery.

"Wait!" Harry said. "I know a *different* recipe for making volcanoes. My grandma showed me."

"Do I have the ingredients?" Miss Mackle asked, opening up her cabinet. "I keep bags of sugar for making crystals, and salt and flour for relief maps."

Mary crossed her fingers.

"I only need *one* ingredient," Harry said. "Flour. And *one* tool. A straw."

Then he reached for a cafeteria lunch tray that was on the counter and set it on the empty table in front of the room.

We watched Harry dump the *entire* bag of flour in the tray. "You need *all of it?*" Miss Mackle checked.

"Yup. But you can use it again after our experiment."

The teacher nodded slowly. "O-kay."

"Ready to build a mighty volcano, Mare?"

"Yes, Harry," Mary replied, standing tall and proud.

"Start patting," he ordered. "Gently!"

We watched the two of them pat, pat, pat the sides until they made a big flour mountain.

"Mary will make a chute down the center," Harry announced, handing her the straw.

Mary slowly poked, poked, poked. Then she passed the straw back to her partner.

"Now," Harry explained, "I shall drill a tunnel from the side that connects with the central chute."

Miss Mackle stepped behind Harry, and watched over his shoulders.

"Okay," Harry said. "Everyone ready?"

"Ready!" we all shouted.

Harry put the straw next to his lips and stuck the other end into the side tunnel. Then he blew and blew and blew.

Poof!

Out came a *huge puff of white smoke!*

It looked like a giant cumulus cloud in Room 3B.

"Whoa!" everyone said as they watched the cloud move up, up, up.

Suddenly the cloud rained tiny white specks! Right on Harry and Mary and Miss Mackle! They looked like they had been dropped in a flour bin. Their eyebrows and eyelashes and hair were all caked in white powder.

Just then, Mr. Marks, the music teacher, walked in singing his usual "La ti dah, ti dah." As soon as he saw the three flour heads, he stopped, and laughed with the rest of us.

Except for Mary. She didn't think it was funny. She was so mad she blew her bangs up, but when she did, she got more flour in her face.

Mr. Marks gave everyone the A-Okay sign. "I've heard of *hands*-on science, but I like what you guys did better. *Heads*-on science."

Then he gave Miss Mackle a wink.

Harry's Discovery

As soon as we cleaned up the flour fallout, Mr. Marks gave us our recorders. We practiced "Row, Row, Row Your Boat," five times. Usually Miss Mackle leaves the room when we practice, but she stayed at her desk and watched this time.

After music, I asked Miss Mackle if I could go next door and ask Mr. Skooghammer to fix our computer. "I want to go to FactMonster.com and get more facts about volcanoes."

"What a good idea!" the teacher said.

"Can I go with Doug?" Harry begged. "We need to know what's on the other side of our closet. It might be helpful for our detective work."

Then Harry flashed a toothy smile.

"Okay, Harry." I could tell Miss Mackle was in a good mood.

Halfway down the hall, Harry stopped to pull out his pocket notebook. "Who is *that* guy?" Harry asked, pointing to a picture on the wall. "We walk by him every day."

I read the tiny print underneath. "It says he was principal at South School from 1960 to 1985. His name is Mr. Stromboli."

"Stromboli?" Harry replied. "That's

the name of a famous volcano in Italy.
Mary and I read about it."

"No kidding?" I said as Harry jotted
it down.

When we got to the computer room,
we waited in the doorway. Mr. Skooghammer was helping a few students
run their program.

He was a cool teacher. When he supervised the suspension room last June, he had an earring in his eyebrow. But when he got hired after Christmas to be the computer teacher, he didn't have it.

As soon as he saw us, he came over. "Hey partners, what brings you into my neck of the woods?"

"Our computer is frozen," I replied. "What should we do?"

"Pull the plug," he said. "Then restart it."

"I thought so," I said.

Harry was already in the corner by the window, investigating the closet.

Mr. Skooghammer followed him. "Looking for something, Harry?"

"I'm investigating the biggest mystery ever at South School," Harry explained.

"Our closet has been locked for years! No one knows what's inside! I'm trying to get clues by looking at your closet. It's *directly* behind ours!"

Mr. Skooghammer started to laugh. "You're investigating the General's closet?"

"The General?" we repeated.

"That's what we called him. He was an officer in the Korean War. His name was Mr. Stromboli. He taught in Room 3B. When I went here, he was the principal. His picture is in the hallway."

Harry and I both nodded.

"The kids called him 'The General' because he was so strict. He made South School feel like a fort. He never walked down the hall. He marched."

"I wonder why he locked his closet?" Harry asked.

"It may have been locked by the custodian. When Mr. Stromboli became principal, they made Room 3B into a music room. They parked a piano in front of your locked closet and left it there until last summer."

"Whoa," I said. "That means our closet has been locked for almost forty-five years!"

Mr. Skooghammer put two thumbs up. "Good math work, Doug!" he said. "The piano was moved to the kindergarten last fall when your class moved up to third grade. We don't have space for a music room now."

"What do you think is inside the General's closet?" Harry asked eagerly.

"There were rumors about that, too," Mr. Skooghammer said. "Kids used to say Mr. Stromboli kept his military

supplies in that closet, and if you were bad, he would make you sit on his hard army helmet for an hour in the corner."

Then Mr. Skooghammer laughed.

"Did *you* ever have to sit on his hard army helmet?" I asked.

"No. But he did punish me once. He caught me running in the hall, and made me march up and down the stairs ten times. After that, I never ran in the hall."

Mr. Skooghammer pulled on his beard. "My neighbor had Mr. Stromboli for a teacher. I always wondered why he never complained about him. Unfortunately, my neighbor moved away last year. Go ahead and take a look in my closet. I'm sure it's just like yours. I have to get back to my small group."

Harry and I said thanks, then opened the closet door. Just as we stepped inside, I felt a tap on my shoulder. It made me jump!

"Mary!" I said. "What are you doing here?"

"Miss Mackle sent me to get you. She wanted to know what was taking you so long."

Harry lowered his eyebrows. "Detective work takes time."

Mary weaseled her way in front of Harry. "Just boring stuff in this closet," she said. "Boots, a winter coat . . ."

"Computer programs, a push broom," I added. "You're right. Let's go. I don't want to get in trouble."

"Me, either," Mary agreed.

We walked quickly to the door, thanked Mr. Skooghammer, and went

back to Room 3B. Halfway down the hall, we realized Harry wasn't with us, so we waited.

Twenty *long* seconds later, Harry appeared. "You guys missed two things," he said.

"What *two things?*" Mary replied.

"You'll find out when I tell the class."

I made a face. I wanted to know now.

The Hole in the Closet

Miss Mackle wasn't smiling when she greeted us at the door. "What took you so long? You were gone almost ten minutes!"

"Good detective work takes time," Harry said proudly. "We got the scoop on our locked closet from Mr. Skooghammer. He used to go to school here."

"No kidding!" Ida replied.

"Yeah," Harry continued. "Our closet

was locked years ago when he was a kid. They even had a name for it. The General's closet."

"The General's closet! Why?" ZuZu quizzed. Harry filled everyone in on the military details. Finally he got to the part Mary and I were waiting for.

"So today when I was checking out the computer closet, I made a huge discovery."

"What?" everyone gasped.

"A trapdoor in the ceiling!"

"Oooooh!" the class replied.

"Just like the one in my grandma's closet," Harry explained. "I bet it opens up to the attic, too."

Miss Mackle wasn't frowning anymore. She was curious like us. "Maybe there's a trapdoor in our locked closet!"

"I think we should have a search

committee go up to the attic and see," Mary declared. "Harry should go because he was the one who discovered the trapdoor. Doug should go because he's Harry's assistant, and I should go because I'm the messenger this week."

"Sounds like a good idea, Mary," Miss Mackle agreed. "And I'll ask Mr. Skooghammer to go with the search party tomorrow at noon, because I unfortunately have lunch duty."

The teacher reached for her big jar of class names. "Now, I think to be fair I should add another girl to the search party."

Miss Mackle called out the first girl's name she drew. "Song Lee."

Song Lee clapped her hands and giggled with joy.

Then something happened at the pencil sharpener that made things even more exciting. Harry tiptoed up behind me and whispered, "There's something *else* I saw in the computer closet. Something behind Mr. Skooghammer's coat."

"What?" I whispered back.

"A *hole* in the wall, the size of a golf ball."

"A *hole?*"

Harry quickly covered my mouth. "Shhh! I'll show you after school."

At 3:05 P.M., when the walkers were dismissed to go home and the bus kids were sent to the bus line, Harry and I scooted into the computer room.

"Hey, what's up?" Mr. Skooghammer said. He was chewing on some beef jerky and reading the newspaper.

"I think I left my notebook in your closet today," Harry said.

"Go check," Mr. Skooghammer replied.

"Thanks," Harry said. Then we darted into the closet. Harry opened his backpack and took out a mini-flashlight.

"I don't like fibbing to a teacher," I whispered.

"I wasn't fibbing," Harry said. "I really did leave my notebook here."

"You did?"

"Sure, detectives plant things all the time." Then he reached into one of Mr. Skooghammer's snow boots and pulled out his notebook. "See?"

After Harry made his eyebrows go up and down a few times, he poked the flashlight through the hole in the back of the closet. "Oh, man . . ." he whispered.

"What do you see?"

"A pair of eyeballs."

"*What?*" I gasped.

"Take a look yourself," Harry replied.

I did. They were eyeballs all right. "D-do you think it's Mr. Stromboli's gh-ghost?"

Harry flashed his white teeth and smiled. Then he put his ear in the hole. "It sounds like the ghost is talking . . ."

I took two steps back.

Harry's eyeballs orbited around in his sockets as he listened. It was the longest fifteen seconds ever! Finally, Harry walked out of the closet holding his notebook.

"Great!" Mr. Skooghammer said. "You found it!"

"Yeah," I said, answering for Harry. He was speechless.

As soon as we stepped into the hallway, Harry's shoulders slumped. "What I *heard* wasn't a ghost, Doug."

I breathed easier. "Phew!"

"It was our teacher's voice."

"Miss Mackle? What did she say?"

"She was talking to some man. I heard her say, 'I can't wait to go . . . to Oklahoma with you.'"

"Oklahoma?" I exclaimed. "That's a different state a thousand miles away!"

Harry shook his head as we got closer to Room 3B. "Miss Mackle is . . . moving. She's not . . . going to be our . . . teacher anymore."

We took a quick look when we passed

by our room, and saw who the man was.

Mr. Marks.

Miss Mackle was going to Oklahoma with our music teacher!

"What are we going to do?" Harry pleaded.

"There's only one thing to do," I replied. "Follow me."

Harry followed me to the stairwell. I looked both ways. No one else was around, so I sat down on the top step, bowed my head, and said a silent prayer.

When I looked up, Harry was doing the same thing. It was the first time Harry and I had ever prayed together.

The Search Party
in the Attic

The next day when the morning bell rang, Harry and I raced up the stairs to our classroom. Mr. Skooghammer was already there talking to our teacher.

"Yes, I'm going to Oklahoma tonight," Miss Mackle said.

"Wonderful!" Mr. Skooghammer replied.

Wonderful? Harry stopped in his tracks at the doorway. Now he had heard it for a *second* time! It was true, but it was *not* wonderful!

"Hi boys!" Mr. Skooghammer said when he saw us. "I think it's so cool you discovered the trapdoor in my closet. I never noticed!"

I nodded.

Harry tied both sneakers. He didn't want anyone to see how upset he was.

"So, guys," Mr. Skooghammer said. "I'll stop by at noon, and take your search party up to the attic. We're about to unlock the General's closet!"

"I'm glad you're coming with us," I gulped.

Mr. Skooghammer laughed. "I wouldn't miss it. This mystery goes back to my childhood days!" Then he and Miss Mackle stepped into the hallway and chatted more about Oklahoma.

As soon as we sat down, Mary made

a beeline over to Harry's desk. "Harry Spooger, you've been acting funny ever since you came to school this morning. I think you're hiding something."

Harry gritted his teeth.

"If it's about our locked closet, you must tell me now! I'm in the search party too, you know!"

"Okay," Harry snarled, "you want to know what else I found out?"

Mary took a step back and nodded. The class turned to listen.

"I saw a hole in the closet!"

"No way!" she gasped. "I was there. I would have seen it."

"Well you missed it, Mare. It was underneath Mr. Skooghammer's winter coat. And when I looked through the hole into our locked closet, I saw . . ." Harry's voice boomed, *"eyeballs!"*

"Aaauuuugh!" the class shrieked.

Miss Mackle immediately stepped back into the room. "Boys and girls, you are so noisy!"

"Harry is making up stories about our closet!" Mary tattled. "He's trying to scare us."

Miss Mackle gave Harry a look.

Harry shrugged. Mary returned to her seat. The rest of us turned pin quiet.

Finally, after a long morning, it was noon. Mr. Beausoleil, our custodian, Mr. Cardini, our principal, and Mr. Skooghammer took Harry and Mary and Song Lee and me up to the attic. The search party walked single file up the narrow, winding squeaky stairwell.

Mr. Cardini was the first to speak. "So, your closet is close to being a forty-five year time capsule!"

"Yes!" Mary, Song Lee, and I replied.

Mr. Cardini looked at Harry. "You're awfully quiet today!"

"Harry wasn't quiet this morning," Mary tattled. "He yelled at me!"

"Is that right, Harry?" the principal asked.

Harry made an effort to smile for Mr. Cardini. But I knew it was a cover-up. Harry had lost all interest in the biggest mystery in Room 3B.

When we got to the top of

the stairs, Mr. Beausoleil switched on another set of lights. The school attic was huge! It covered the entire second floor of South School.

We followed him across the wooden floor. There were boxes, crates, and desks everywhere. "Look at all the broken kindergarten chairs," Mary said.

"Over here." Mr. Beausoleil pointed. "Here's the trapdoor to the closet in the computer room."

Mr. Beausoleil and Mr. Skooghammer moved a heavy box of textbooks toward the wall.

"Looky here!" Mr. Skooghammer exclaimed. "There's *one big* trapdoor right over the computer room closet *and* Room 3B's closet!"

Mr. Cardini fiddled with his mustache. "I bet those two closets below were originally one big one."

"I think so," Mr. Beausoleil replied. "That would explain why the back wall is so thin. I noticed it when I accidentally poked a hole in it with my broom handle last week. I've been meaning to fix it."

Mary covered her mouth! I knew what she was thinking. If Harry's story about the hole was true, was the story about the eyeballs true, too?

"Well," Mr. Cardini said, "should we open up the trapdoor now or let Mr. Beausoleil check things out first?"

Suddenly, a tiny bat flew out from the far corner of the attic. As it flapped its wings overhead, Mary and I screamed. Song Lee giggled. Harry just stood still.

He wasn't worried about any little bat.

"That bat just answered my question, kids," Mr. Cardini said. "Let's go

downstairs and leave the rest of the investigation to Mr. Beausoleil. If it's safe to do so, he can enter the locked closet through the trapdoor and open it up for you."

Not one of us objected. We hurried back down the stairs looking very relieved. Harry just had a very long face. He was worried about losing his favorite teacher.

The Mystery Is Solved!

Dear Miss Mackle
I'll miss You
very very very
very very very
very very very

That afternoon, we waited for Mr. Beausoleil to open up our locked closet. Room 3B even had two visitors. Mrs. Michaelsen and Mr. Skooghammer. Everyone was psyched!

Except for Harry. He was putting the finishing touches on his farewell card for the teacher. It said "I'll Miss You Very Much" with twenty-one "verys." Right now he was drawing black ants carrying red hearts in the border.

"Miss Mackle," Sidney asked, "what's keeping Mr. Beausoleil?"

"He's rounding up a chain ladder so he can climb down from the trapdoor in the attic."

I looked at the clock. It was 2:05 P.M.

"Boys and girls," Mr. Cardini said, rushing into the room, "is the mystery closet open yet?"

"No!" we all replied.

"Bravissimo! I was at a meeting and it was hard to get away. I don't want to miss anything! So, what do you boys and girls think is in that locked closet?"

"Eyeballs," everyone volunteered.

"Eyeballs?" the principal replied.

"Listen, everybody!" ZuZu exclaimed. "I hear somebody in the closet!"

We all leaned forward in our seats

and kept our eyes on the closet door.

There was a *creak, creak, creak.*

Harry even looked up from his farewell card.

"It's Mr. Beausoleil!" Sidney blurted out. "He's coming down the chain ladder."

The creaking got louder.

"Boom!" A noise sounded from the closet.

"He landed!" ZuZu shouted.

The black doorknob slowly turned counterclockwise.

"Click!" The mystery door swung wide open!

We all saw the same thing.

"Mr. Stromboli!" we shouted.

There on the inside of the closet door was a big picture of Mr. Stromboli in his army uniform. I sighed as I sank down

in my chair. So *that's* what we saw! Mr. Stromboli's eyeballs on the picture!

Phew! I thought.

Everyone cheered and clapped as the custodian stepped out of the closet. "That closet was well sealed off," Mr. Beausoleil announced. "I checked everything out. Hardly any dust. Just a few dust balls on the floor that rolled in from my daily sweeping. There were a couple of amazing cobwebs in the corners, but I took care of them with my mop."

Miss Mackle stepped in and quickly eyeballed the inside of the closet. "I don't believe it, boys and girls!" she said, twirling around. "After almost forty-five years, you're going to see what's in the General's closet. I mean Mr. Stromboli's closet. I'm going to let each one of you come inside, one by one. Choose one thing that catches your eye and set it on this long table in front of the room for everyone to see!"

Mr. Cardini twirled his mustache and snorted, he was so excited.

"Harry," the teacher said, "I want you to go first. This whole closet idea was yours to begin with!"

Harry jumped out of his seat and ran to the teacher. He gave her the biggest and longest hug.

"Why, Harry!" Miss Mackle said. "You're just full of enthusiasm, aren't you! See what you can find."

Harry was so worried about the teacher, he didn't explore at all. He just reached for the push broom in the corner and set it on the table.

Everyone laughed but Harry.

I noticed when he went back to his seat that his eyes were filling up with tears. There was so much going on though, no one else noticed.

Mary went next. She pulled out a View-Master with three disks, and blew off a little dust. "Maybe there's one about volcanoes!" she said. "I'm going to check and see!"

Dexter brought out some Illustrated Junior Classic comic books. "These are cool!" he said, looking at one that had a whale on the cover.

Ida pulled out a wooden beanbag toss that stood up like a sawhorse and had three holes.

Song Lee brought out a jump rope with red handles.

I carried out an Erector set.

Sidney picked up the Tinker Toys.

"I'm making a canary!" Then he looked at Harry, trying to make him laugh.

But Harry didn't.

ZuZu chose the wooden Lincoln Logs. "I'll have to keep these away from Ju-Ju. He'll gnaw right through them!"

Miss Mackle reached up to the highest shelf and brought down a box of books. "Look at these, boys and girls!"

Mary rooted through the box first, and pulled out ones she knew. "I've read these!" she exclaimed. "I want to read them again!"

"Me, too!" Song Lee, ZuZu, and Ida replied.

"We call them classics," Mrs. Michaelsen said. "Stories that have been enjoyed for fifty years or more!"

Then she helped us stack our favorites along the windowsill of Room 3B: *Millions of Cats, Stone Soup, Madeline, Make Way for Ducklings, The Story of Babar, Curious George, The Story about Ping, The Five Chinese Brothers, My Father's Dragon, Henry Huggins, Charlotte's Web, Mr. Popper's Penguins, The Story of Ferdinand,* and *Homer Price.*

In the next ten minutes, board games were displayed on the long table: Candy Land, Monopoly, Scrabble, and Clue!

I opened up the box that the Monopoly game came in. "Look at this!" I said. "The red hotels and green houses aren't plastic. They're all wooden!"

"Take a look at this 1949 version of Clue," Mr. Skooghammer said. After he examined the real rope and the tiny metal weapons, he held up one of the suspect cards. "Colonel Mustard looks like you, Mr. Cardini."

Mr. Cardini admired the mustache on the man and chuckled. "Handsome fellow!"

Then Mr. Skooghammer made an announcement. "You know, boys and girls, I learned something about the General. He had a things-to-do closet that was fun! No wonder my neighbor never complained about him. Don't ever pay attention to rumors. I wish I hadn't. There are no military helmets in this closet!"

"Next time we have indoor recess, we'll have plenty of fun things to do!" Mary said. "Thanks to Mr. Stromboli! I never knew we would like the same things kids did fifty years ago!"

"If it's a really good book or a really good toy, it will last!" Mrs. Michaelsen replied.

"A really good song lasts, too," Mr. Marks added from the doorway. Then he took a turn and walked into our mystery closet.

Harry and I waited and watched. He and Miss Mackle were probably going to make an announcement about leaving any minute now.

"Hey," Mr. Marks called as he carried something out of the closet. "Look what I found, Miss Mackle!"

Our teacher looked over, and so did

everyone else. "An old book of songs from Broadway plays from the forties. Some of my favorite tunes are here. Even—"

"'Oklahoma'?" Miss Mackle asked.

"Yes!" And then Mr. Marks started to sing, "'Ooooooklahoma where the wind comes sweeping down the plains!'"

Harry ran up to the teacher. "Oklahoma is a *song?*"

"Yes. But it's also a musical," Miss Mackle explained. "We're going to see it tonight at the Warner Theater."

Mary and Song Lee both giggled.

Harry and I jumped in the air slapping each other ten. Our teacher wasn't moving. She was just . . . going on a date!

Miss Mackle shrugged as she smiled at Mr. Marks.

Harry wadded up his farewell card and slam-dunked it into the garbage can. When he paused a moment to close his eyes, I knew he was saying a secret prayer. I did, too. We were thankful that everything turned out okay.

Harry then made a beeline to the detective game on the long table. "Miss

Mackle, can we play Clue?" he asked. "Please?"

The teacher looked up at the wall clock. "It's after 2:30 P.M. There isn't much time left in our day, and we should celebrate finding all these treasures in our closet. Go ahead!"

"Dibs on being Colonel Mustard!" Mr. Cardini said. "I don't have another meeting until after school."

"Dibs on being Miss Scarlet!" Mr. Skooghammer joked. "Lucky me, this is my planning time!"

Miss Mackle and Mrs. Michaelsen helped kids get started with the other board games. Mr. Beausoleil lined up a group of us for beanbag tossing. "I used to play this all the time!" he said.

ZuZu and Sidney started building a

Ferris wheel out of Tinker Toys.

JuJu gnawed on his big block of wood.

Everyone was doing something.

I smiled ear to ear.

While the class had discovered what was inside the closet, I had discovered what was going on outside.

The most important thing to Harry in Room 3B was *not* something horrible at all.

It was something very nice.

Our teacher, Miss Mackle.

And that was the biggest surprise of all!

(Don't tell anyone.)

Appendix

Song Lee and Doug's Volcano Facts

1. A person who studies a volcano is a volcanologist.

2. All volcanoes release steam and gases.

3. Not all volcanoes produce lava.

4. Magma is molten rock inside the volcano.

5. Magma rumbles and roars.

6. When magma erupts and falls outside the volcano, it's called lava.

7. Basalt is the most common rock formed from lava.

8. The Ring of Fire refers to a large circle around the Pacific Ocean where almost half of the world's volcanoes are located.

9. The word *volcano* comes from Vulcan, the Roman god of fire.

10. There are three kinds of volcanoes: active, dormant, and extinct.

11. Volcanoes have three shapes: shield, composite, and cinder cone.

Room 3B's
Volcano Recipe

(Make sure to ask an adult before you begin.)

INGREDIENTS:

one empty quart juice bottle

cookie tray

water

baking soda

white vinegar

liquid dishwashing detergent

red food coloring

DIRECTIONS:

1. Pour one cup of water into the bottle.
2. Place it in the middle of a cookie tray.
3. Add two tablespoons of baking soda.
4. Add two squirts of detergent.

5. Add twelve drops of red food coloring.
6. Pour in one cup of white vinegar.

Stand back and watch the *explosion!*

The baking soda and vinegar make carbon dioxide. The carbon dioxide creates the foam and forces the liquid out of the bottle.